The Maybe GArden

Kimberly Burke-Weiner
Author

Fredrika Spillman
Illustrations

Beyond Words Publishing, Inc.

Beyond Words Publishing, Inc.
13950 NW Pumpkin Ridge Rd.
Hillsboro, OR 97123
(503) 647-5109

Printed in Mexico

Library of Congress Cataloging-in-Publication Data

Burke-Weiner, Kimberly, 1962- .
      The maybe garden/Kimberly Burke-Weiner, author ; Fredrika.
  Spillman, illustrations.
          p.   cm.
      Summary: A child uses Mother's ordinary suggestions for a garden
  as a springboard for imagining all sorts of unique and creative
  garden ideas.
      ISBN 0-941831-56-6 (hard) : $14.95 — ISBN 0-941831-57-4 (soft) :
  $7.95
      [1. Gardens — Fiction.   2. Imagination — Fiction.   3. Individuality —
  Fiction.]   I. Spillman, Fredrika, 1938-   ill.   II. Title.
  PZ7.B9224May 1992
  [Fic] — dc20   92-7452
                                                                  CIP
                                                                  AC

My first for my only.
Kim

To Toby who is my teacher.
Fredrika

She has the most immaculate garden in the world, my mother.

Her friends sit on the bench and smell the rows of flowers and
say how lovely and straight the garden is. They drink tea and freeze
when the bees buzz around the lemon slices on their saucers.

The neighbors peek over the fence and ask how to prune their
roses and how far apart tulips should be and if sweet peas grow
better in sun or shade.

I am going to plant my own garden.

My mother says, "*Maybe you should plant an avocado seed and watch it grow into a tree.*"

Maybe I will.

Maybe I will plant an apple tree and tie balloons to all the apples
so that when they are ripe they will fall softly to the ground.

"*Maybe you should plant a neat little row of daisies,*"
my mother says.

Maybe I will.

Maybe I'll plant three rows of sunflowers and put up a beach umbrella. I'll get some sand from the beach and spread it under the umbrella. I'll put out some big shells for listening to the ocean.

"*Or how about pansies? They grow well.*"

Maybe.

Maybe I'll plant peanuts. Then I'll build a huge elephant statue out of rocks. I'll paint it pink and purple and white. Birds will sit on its back.

"*How about marigolds? They keep snails away.*"

Maybe.

Maybe I'll plant strawberries and invite the snails to live among them. I'll make tiny pink and silver houses so that the fairies can live there too.

"*A row of tomatoes would be nice. How about planting tomatoes?*"

Maybe I will.

Maybe I'll plant one hundred carrots and let bunnies come and eat them. I'll paint a sign that says "Rabbits welcome." I'll plant clover and write "Deer welcome." I'll plant blackberries and paint "Bears welcome — but don't eat the deer or rabbits."

"Would you like to plant a row of poppies?"

Maybe I would. Maybe I'll plant orange poppies and red snapdragons and yellow buttercups and blue asters and purple violets.

They will bloom into a rainbow. I'll put lanterns around the edges so I can see the rainbow even at night. I've never seen a rainbow at night.

My mother has the most immaculate garden in the world.

Yet mine is the most enchanting.

My friends sit on the elephant and smell the rainbow and listen to tiny oceans and drink apple juice and freeze when the fairies land on their faces.

The neighbors peek through the sunflowers and ask where to get waterfall rocks and what kind of leaves giraffes like and if they may use my sparkle paint.

My mother is digging up part of her garden.

I say, "Maybe you should make a big hole and fill it with water. Put giant goldfish and frogs in it. Float water lilies on the water for the frogs to rest their legs on when they are tired of swimming."

She says, "*Maybe I will.*"

GROWING WILD: Inviting Wildlife into Your Yard
Author/Illustrator: Constance Perenyi
40 pages, $14.95 hardbound, $9.95 softbound, ages 6-9

A story chronicling the changes of a suburban neighborhood from perfectly groomed lawns to a nature-friendly environment. With pages at the back of the book which explain the gardening/ ecological principles in the story, this book introduces young readers to the concept of gardening for wildlife. Illustrated with images crafted of cut and torn paper. Printed on high-quality recycled paper.

DAVY'S DREAM: A Young Boy's Adventure with Wild Orca Whales
Author/Illustrator: Paul Owen Lewis
60 pages, $14.95 hardbound, $9.95 softbound, ages 5-10

The story of a boy who dreams of himself sailing among a pod of wild Orca, or killer whales. The dream is so real he feels he has become a part of their world. Excited by his vision, he sets out to realize his dream. Davy learns that dreams pursued can come true!

P. BEAR'S NEW YEARS PARTY

Author/Illustrator: Paul Owen Lewis
29 pages, $12.95 hardbound, $8.95 softbound, ages 3-6

Designed to teach beginning readers basic counting, this imaginative narrative tells how Mr. P. (Polar) Bear decides to throw a formal New Year's party and invites all his "best-dressed" friends, each sporting a black bow tie. Strikingly presented in black-and-white graphics.

THE STARLIGHT BRIDE

Author/Illustrator: Paul Owen Lewis
36 pages, $14.95 hardbound, $9.95 softbound, ages 7-14

A tale of true love. A young prince must marry before Christmas Day in order to become king. He calls upon his greatest strengths, his faith, his confidence, and his ultimate belief in love to help him in his search for a special young woman. In a magical, mysterious, and romantic turn of events, the prince's faith and determination is rewarded in a way no one could have imagined.

COYOTE STORIES FOR CHILDREN: Tales from Native America

Author: Susan Strauss; Illustrator: Gary Lund
50 pages, $10.95 hardbound, $6.95 softbound, ages 6-12

Storyteller Susan Strauss has interspersed Native American coyote tales with true-life anecdotes about coyotes and Native wisdom. These stories illustrate the creative and foolish nature of this popular trickster and show the wisdom in Native American humor. Whimsical illustrations throughout.

CEREMONY IN THE CIRCLE OF LIFE

Author: White Deer of Autumn; Illustrator: Daniel San Souci
32 pages, $6.95 softbound, ages 6-10

The story of nine-year-old Little Turtle, a young Native American boy growing up in the city without knowledge of his ancestors' beliefs. He is visited by "Star Spirit," who introduces him to his heritage and his relationship to all things in the "Circle of Life." Little Turtle also learns about nature and how he can help to heal the Earth.

THE GREAT CHANGE

Author: White Deer of Autumn; Illustrator: Carol Grigg
32 pages, $14.95 hardbound, ages 3-10

A Native American tale in which a wise grandmother explains the meaning of death, or the Great Change, to her questioning granddaughter. This is a story of passing on tradition, culture, and wisdom to the next generation. It is a moving tale for everyone who wonders about what lies beyond this life. Watercolor illustrations by internationally acclaimed painter Carol Grigg.

ABOUT THE AUTHOR

Kimberly Burke-Weiner is a first-grade teacher in Tacoma, Washington. She hopes someday to be a full-time writer. When Kimberly was a little girl, someone asked her what she'd like to be when she grew up. "Maybe a ballerina or a doctor," she answered. More recently, someone asked her about writing a children's book. She said, "Maybe I will."

It took Kimberly 28 years and three hours to write *The Maybe Garden*. For 28 years she struggled with everyone telling her what to do. Then she wrote a story about it in three hours. People still tell her what to do, but now she doesn't listen very often.

ABOUT THE ILLUSTRATOR

Fredrika Spillman studied sculpture at Rhode Island School of Design and received her bachelor of fine arts degree at Pacific Northwest College of Art. Professionally, she has done free-lance illustration, courtroom drawing, editorial illustration, and book covers for the "Walt Morey Adventure Series."

This is her first children's picture book. Illustrating this book has fulfilled her love of fine art, illustration, and children. She and her husband live on a farm in Oregon and have three children.

SCHOOL PROGRAMS

Kimberly travels the country giving talks and slide presentations on the making of *The Maybe Garden*, while Fredrika does the same in the Pacific Northwest. In their presentations they nourish children's creativity and individuality, encouraging them to take their own unique ideas and say "Maybe I will." If you are interested in having the author or illustrator visit your group, please contact:

Beyond Words Publishing, Inc.
13950 NW Pumpkin Ridge Road
Hillsboro, Oregon 97123
(503) 647-5109